Rebecca Morris

The Rainbow Boat

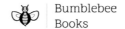
Bumblebee Books

www.olympiapublishers.com

OLYMPIA PAPERBACK EDITION

A CIP catalogue record for this title is
available from the British Library.

ISBN: 978-1-83934-715-3

First Published in 2023

Olympia Publishers
Tallis House
2 Tallis Street
London
EC4Y 0AB

Printed in Great Britain

Dedication

I dedicate this book to my beautiful children.

In a small town by the edge of the sea lived a young boy called Arthur. Arthur lived with his mother, father and brother Henry. Their father was a fisherman, so Arthur and Henry spent a lot of time by the shore helping with the boats and unwinding the fishing nets.

One Sunday afternoon the brothers were helping their father at the shore. As Arthur pulled one of the nets, he saw a gold box no bigger than his hand glisten. He grabbed the box and secretly slid it into his pocket so no one would notice. As the day passed all he could think about was getting home to open the box, his mind fleeting with thoughts of what it could be. Shortly after the family sat down to eat their tea Arthur snook into his room, reaching the small gold box from under his bed. He anxiously opened it to find it was a compass.

"I've never seen anything like this" he muttered to himself before quickly returning to the table.

The following day after school he visited his father down at the shore, as he always does on his walk back home. However, this day was different because he had taken the compass with him, and as he got closer to the sea, he could feel it move in his pocket. Arthur turned away from his father and opened the compass, to find the dials were spinning around.

"Wow" he gasped, leading his father to ask, "wow what Arthur?"

"Nothing father" he quickly replied and slid it back into his coat pocket.

That night Arthur could not sleep and woke his brother Henry to show him what he had found.

"Henry, Henry wake up, I have to show you something."

"Alright, alright what is it" Henry replied.

"I have a magical compass that was spinning around today at the shore."

"Let me see" said Henry in a stern big brother voice.

"That's junk Arthur, its not even spinning."

"It does I swear, it started when I was near the sea."

"Go back to sleep Arthur."

"No ill prove it," said the younger brother. The boys proceeded to get dressed and sneak through the kitchen and out of the back door to walk down onto the shore. The boys sat on the sand at the shoreline patiently waiting for the compass to do something.

"I told you its junk," said Henry.

"Just wait" replied Arthur. When suddenly, the dials started to spin getting faster and faster.

"What the holey moley is that!" shrieked Henry.

The boys stood up when across the horizon they see a huge rainbow coloured boat heading straight towards them.

"I've never seen a boat like that" said Arthur,
"me either" replied Henry.

The brothers were unsure what to do but, at the same time excitement rushed through their bodies as the boat dropped its anchor right in front of them. As the brothers watched on, they saw three pirate looking men walk across the water to them.

"That waters deep, how are they walking on it, what's going on Henry?" the younger brother whispered. Henry just stood gazing in disbelief at the three men walking on water.

As the three men came ashore, Arthur shouted, "are you magic?"

"No dear boy, but that there in your hand is our missing compass. When you opened it, our boat sailed us right to you. Now are you ready for an adventure boys?" The brothers looked at each other not knowing what to say.

"We have to be back by morning," said Arthur.

"No Arthur, we can't go.

"Why have you always got to be so boring Henry,
just one adventure pleaseeee."

"Right ok but we have to be home before mum and
dad notice," replied Henry.

"Right you are boys, you'll be home in no time, follow us.
I'm Diver and this here is Donny and Davey, and we
are the three Gold brothers."

"Nice to meet you," said the brothers. Diver and Donny began rubbing
a gold dust on the boy's boots, "this will get you to the boat, let's go."

"Right ok but we have to be home before mum and dad notice," replied Henry.

"Right you are boys, you'll be home in no time, follow us. I'm Diver and this here is Donny and Davey, and we are the three Gold brothers."

"Nice to meet you," said the brothers. Diver and Donny began rubbing a gold dust on the boy's boots, "this will get you to the boat, let's go."

Arthur and Henry followed the Gold brothers, walking on the water to the boat. "Welcome aboard the rainbow boat," shouted Diver.

"How did we do that?" gasped Henry.

"Well, that is what we call floating dust, you can walk over any water with a bit of that on your shoes." The brothers just starred at each other and then the boat, taking in all her amazing rainbow colours.

"Where are we going" asked Arthur.

"That gold compass is about to take us home thanks to you. We have been slaves of the sea for 22 years while our compass has been missing, we never thought we would see it again."

"Where is your home?" Arthur asked the brothers.

"Far, far away, but your about to find out" replied Davey. The brothers gasped as they saw a huge rainbow in the shape of a triangle in front of the boat. The boat began to set sail towards the triangle rainbow.

"Wait we're going through?" shouted Henry.

"Oh yes we are boys!" replied Diver.

The boat began to speed up and go through the triangle and all you could hear were Arthur and Henry screaming "Ahhhhhhh" when all of a sudden Donny put his arms around the boys and said, "we're here!"

The boys opened their eyes to see the most tropical island they had ever seen. "Welcome to Candy Island boys," said Donny.

Once again, the boys boots were dusted with floating dust and they followed the three Gold brothers to the shore of Candy Island.

This here was no ordinary island. There were animals of all kinds roaming, leaning trees covered in popcorn, slowly popping and falling onto the golden sand.

"Just a short walk over Marshmallow Mountain and we'll be home, follow me," said Diver.

The five set off passing the popping trees towards a forest. Arthur and Henry could not believe their eyes, holding hands the brothers followed into the forest eating handfuls of popcorn as they went. They found themselves crossing a wooden bridge over a red and white stream.

"Careful where you step boys, this here is Candy Cane Creek, it looks tasty buy its very mighty. Anything that drops in sets as hard as a candy cane at Christmas."

The boys struggled and hurried up the mountain. "Can we rest, were so tired?" mumbled Henry. Diver took hold of the gold compass and began to shake it up and down. The young boys both looked up to see a fluffy pink cloud drifting down towards them.

"All aboard the candyfloss cloud, this will take us above the forest to the far side of the Marshmallow Mountain." Said Diver.

"Wowww, this is amazing," said the boys.

They began to fly higher and higher, with the two brothers looking down over Candy Island with amazement.

When they were finally put down by the cloud, they were met with open arms by the island fairies, some flew, some walked and some just floated, but they were so happy and beautiful. The fairy people surrounded the three Gold brothers and gave hugs of happiness as they had finally made their way home.

Arthur and Henry were greeted by giant jelly teddies of all colours filled with tropical juices, bowls full of strawberry puffs and necklaces made from the popcorn trees.

The boys stayed up all night with the Gold brothers and the island fairies eating and drinking all the island had to offer, and listening to the tales of how the fairies raised the three shipwrecked brothers.

The time came for Arthur and Henry to return to their
quiet seaside town and family.

"We will never forget you" said Arthur as the candyfloss cloud
appeared to take them back to the rainbow boat.

"Whenever you feel down or want to smile, just look to the horizon
and remember your adventure on Candy Island," said Davey.

"In every rainbow you see, we'll be watching over you" said Donny.

"And when you dream about the rainbow boat, that will just
be us saying hello," said Diver.

"Thank you for getting us home, we will be forever thankful to you
both Arthur and Henry." The Gold brother's declared.

The boys were taken back to the Rainbow boat on the candyfloss
cloud where they drifted to sleep.

They both woke up at home in their bed like no time had passed at all, to their mother shouting them both for breakfast. As Arthur began to wake up, he turned to Henry and said, "I had the strangest dream last night that we went on an adventure on a rainbow-coloured boat."

Henry looked at his younger brother and said,
"I had the same dream Arthur."

The boys sat down for breakfast and their mother yelled "why on earth are your boots so dusty boys." The brothers smiled and giggled to each other, both knowing their adventures on the Rainbow boat were far from a dream.

The End

"Never be afraid to chase the rainbow."